KT-459-263

# Grandad's Cake and Grandad's Pot

By Lou Treleaven
Illustrated by Natalia Moore

# The Letter X

*Trace the lower and upper case letter with a finger. Sound out the letter.*

*Down,*
*lift,*
*down*

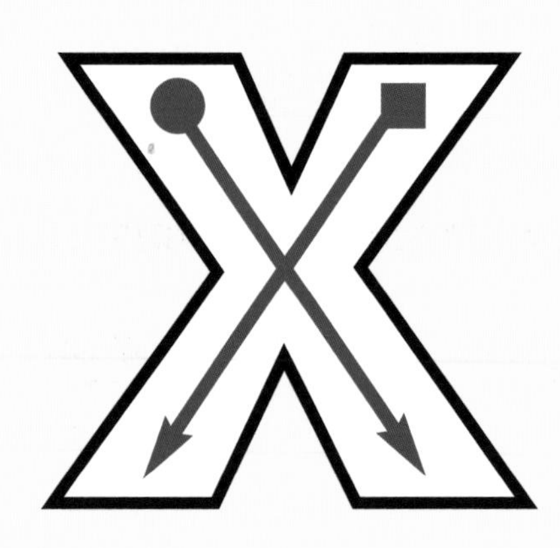

*Down,*
*lift,*
*down*

*Some words to familiarise:*

bake
cake
choc

*High-frequency words:*

we a the to

**Tips for Reading 'Grandad's Cake'**

*- Practise the words listed above before reading the story.*

*- If the reader struggles with any of the other words, ask them to look for sounds they know in the word. Encourage them to sound out the words and help them read the words if necessary.*

*- After reading the story, ask the reader why Grandad and the girl cannot show the cake to Mum.*

**Fun Activity**

*Bake your very own cake.*

# Grandad's Cake

We will bake a cake for Mum.

Flour

Mum must not spot the cake.

Butter

We will mix the cake.

Oops!

Mum must not see the cake.

We will bake the cake. Oops!

Mum must not find the cake.

We will add choc to the cake.

Oops!
Choc

Mum must not see the cake.

We will try the cake.

Yum.

Yum.

Yum.

Yum!

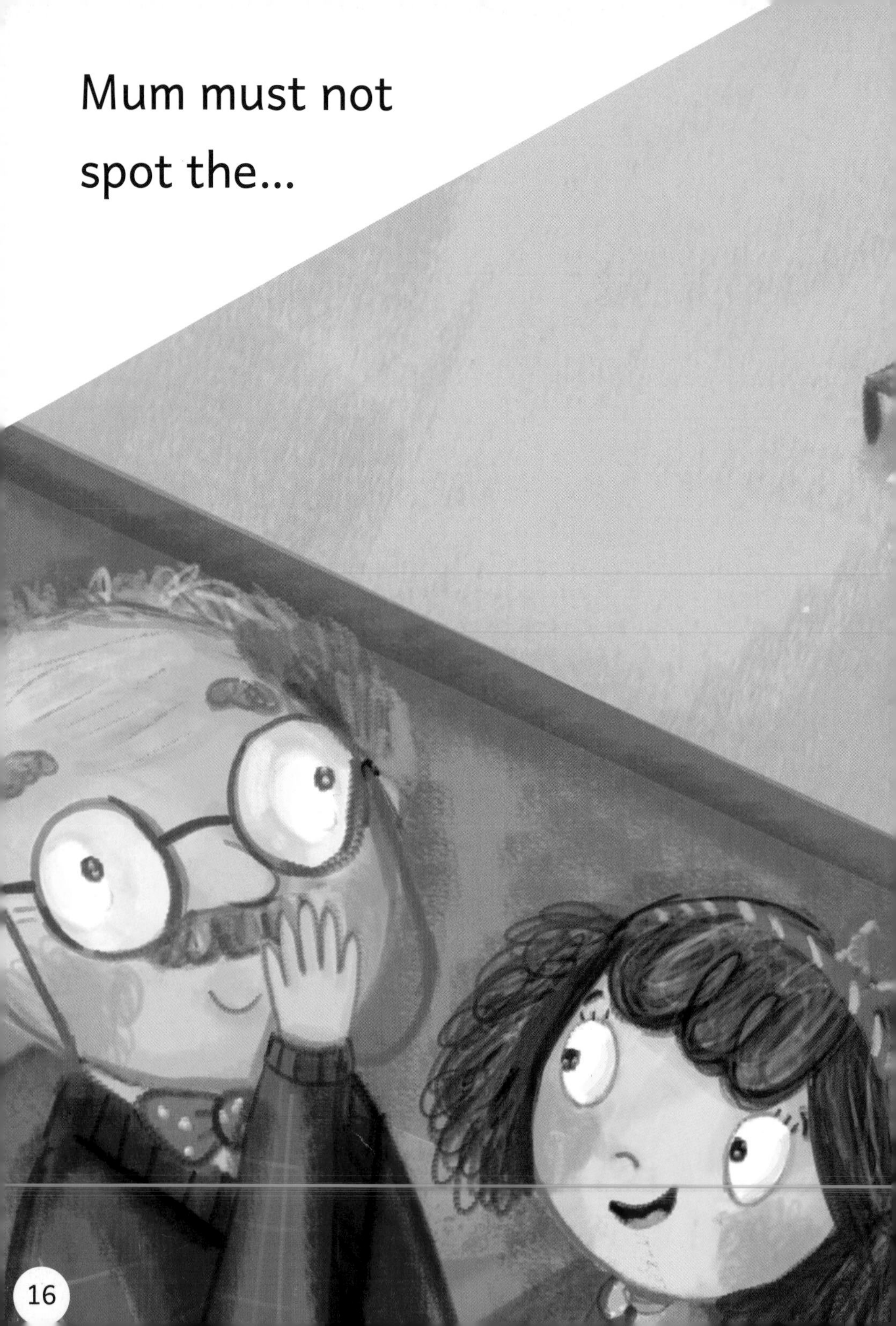

Mum must not
spot the...

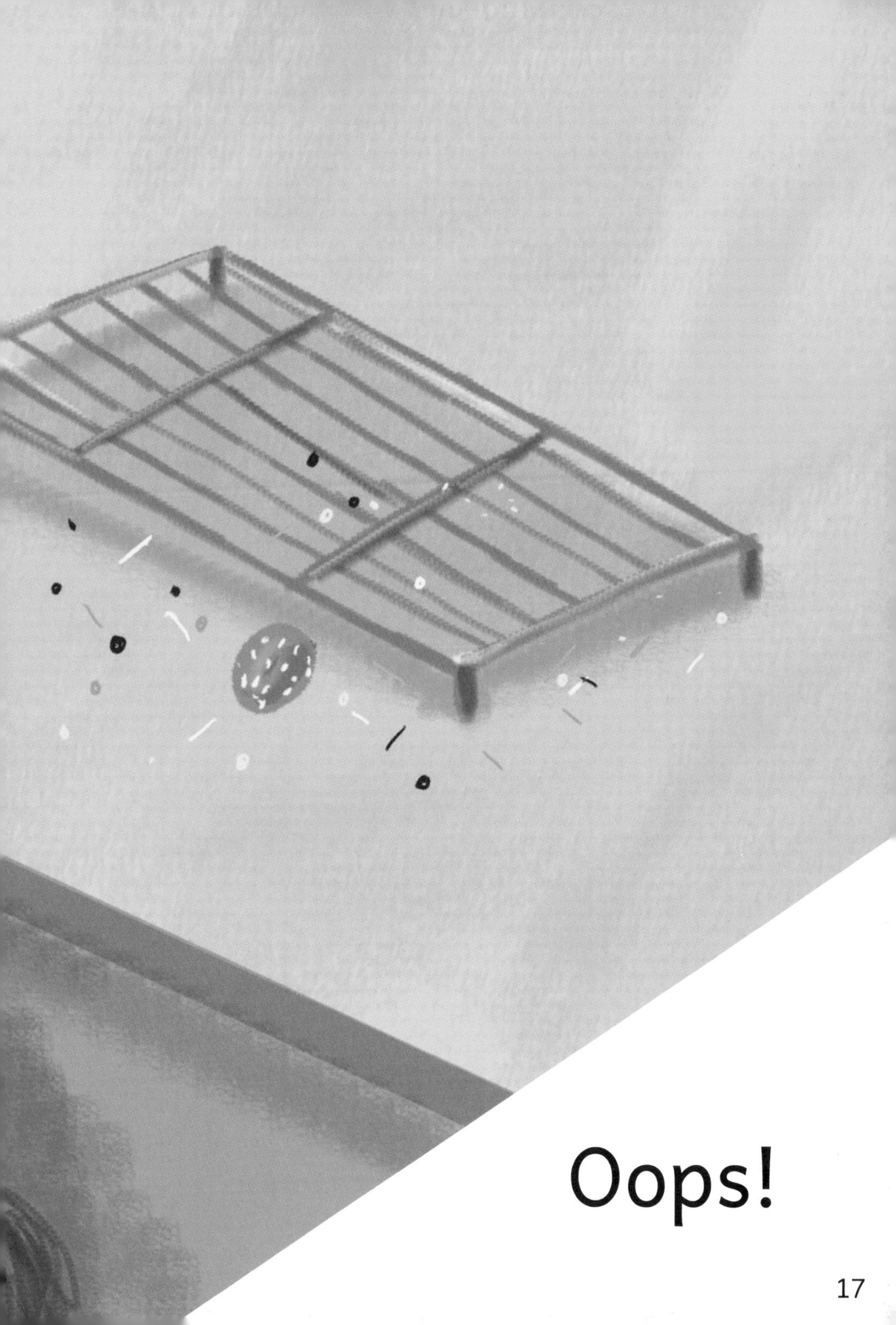

Oops!

# The Letter T

*Trace the lower and upper case letter with a finger. Sound out the letter.*

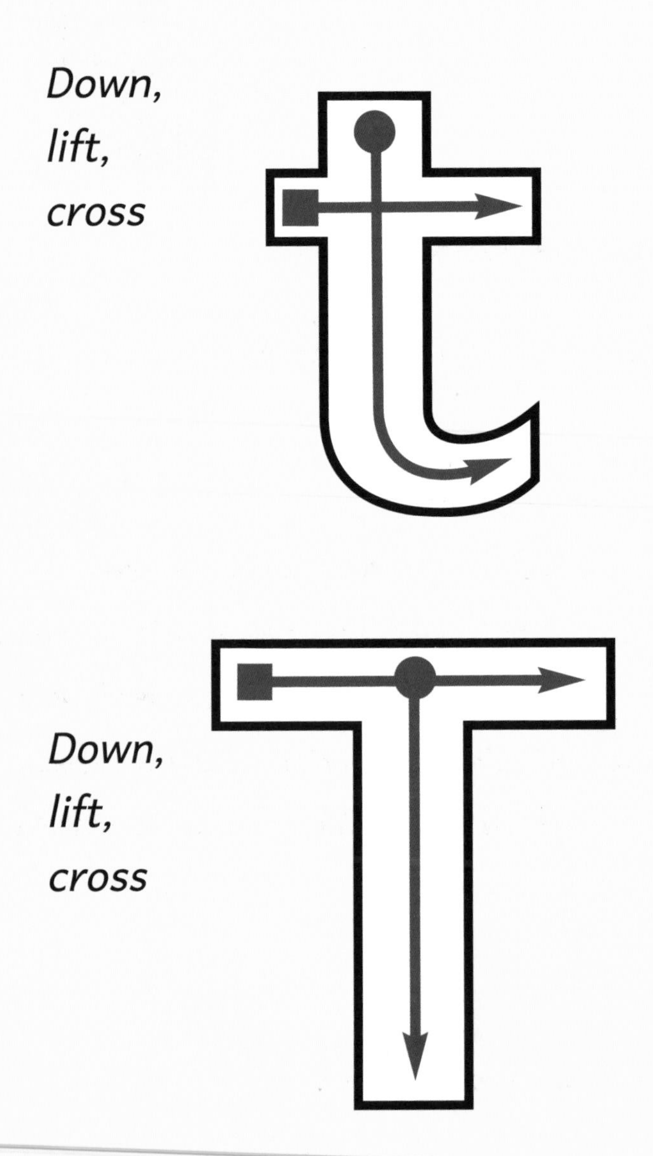

Down,
lift,
cross
Down,
lift,
cross

*Some words to familiarise:*

Grandad

seed

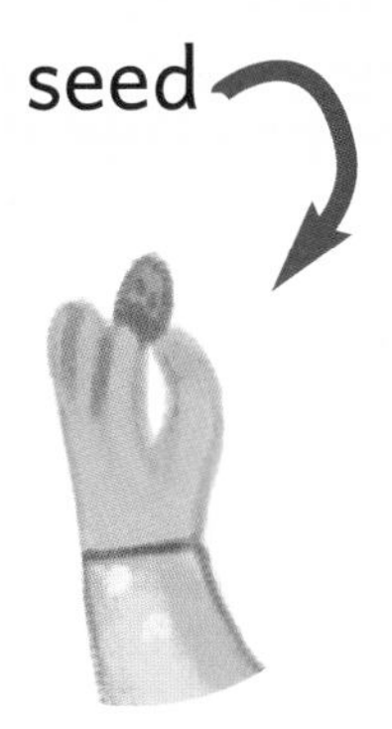

plant

*High-frequency words:*

in a put the

**Tips for Reading 'Grandad's Pot'**

*- Practise the words listed above before reading the story.*

*- If the reader struggles with any of the other words, ask them to look for sounds they know in the word. Encourage them to sound out the words and help them read the words if necessary.*

*- After reading the story, ask the reader what was in Grandad's pot in the end.*

**Fun Activity**

*Plant your own seeds and see what happens.*

# Grandad's Pot

Look in Grandad's pot.

There's not a lot in Grandad's pot.

Put a seed in the pot.

Wait.

There's not a lot in Grandad's pot.

Put water in the pot.

Wait.

There's not a lot in Grandad's pot.

Put the pot in the sun.
Wait.

There's not a lot in Grandad's pot.

Wait. Wait. Wait.

Look in Grandad's pot!

There's a plant
in Grandad's pot!

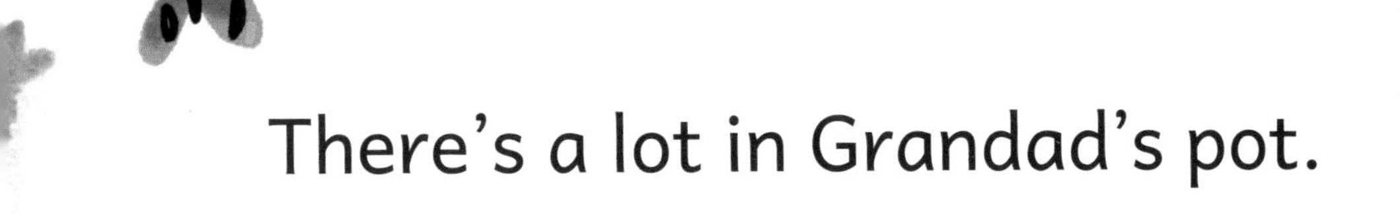

There's a lot in Grandad's pot.

# Book Bands for Guided Reading

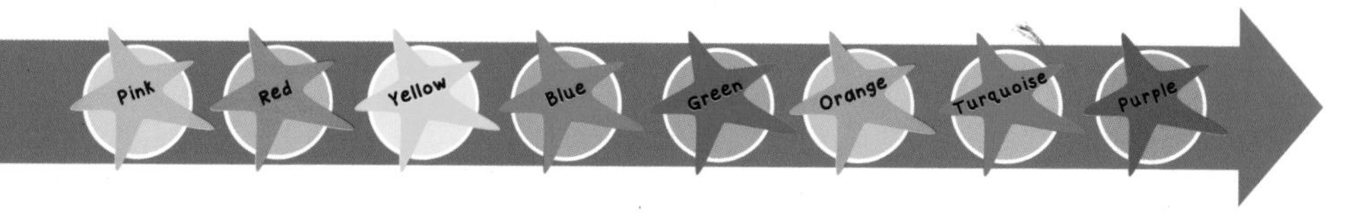
Pink
Red
Yellow
Blue
Green
Orange
Turquoise
Purple

Red
Dog in a Dress and Run, Tom, Run!
978-1-84886-290-6
Buzz and Jump! Jump!
978-1-84886-250-0
Bam-Boo and I Wish
978-1-84886-251-7
Sam the Star and Clown Fun!
978-1-84886-288-3
Seeds and Stuck in the Tree
978-1-84886-289-0
Viv the Vet and Top Dog
978-1-84886-347-7
Go Away! and Let's Make A Rocket
978-1-84886-350-7
Catch It, Jess! and Cat Nap
978-1-84886-348-4
Grandad's Cake and Grandad's Pot
978-1-84886-351-4
Zoom! and Come Back, Mack!
978-1-84886-349-1
Plus many more titles in the scheme!

To view the whole Maverick Readers scheme, please visit:

www.maverickbooks.co.uk/early-readers

The Institute of Education book banding system is a scale of colours that reflects the various levels of reading difficulty. The bands are assigned by taking into account the content, the language style, the layout and phonics.

Maverick Early Readers are a bright, attractive range of books covering the pink to purple bands. All of these books have been book banded for guided reading to the industry standard and edited by a leading educational consultant.